For Lon, who loves umbrellas,
and for Ivy and Ian, the Florida cousins

A.H.

For Natalie and Sophie Lou
my granddaughters

J.B.

First published 1995 by Walker Books Ltd
87 Vauxhall Walk, London SE11 5HJ

2 4 6 8 10 9 7 5 3 1

Text © 1995 Amy Hest
Illustrations © 1995 Jill Barton

This book has been typeset in OPTI Lucius Ad Bold.

Printed in Italy

British Library Cataloguing in Publication Data
A catalogue record for this book is available
from the British Library.

ISBN 0-7445-4035-6

In the Rain
with
Baby Duck

written by **Amy Hest**

illustrated by **Jill Barton**

WALKER BOOKS
AND SUBSIDIARIES
LONDON • BOSTON • SYDNEY

P*it-pat.*

    Pit-a-pat.

Pit-a-pit-a-pat.

Oh, the rain came down.

It poured and poured.

Baby Duck was cross.

She did not like walking in the rain.

But it was Pancake Sunday, a Duck family

tradition, and Baby loved pancakes.

And she loved Grandpa, who was waiting

on the other side of town.

Pit-pat. Pit-a-pat. Pit-a-pit-a-pat.

"Follow us! Step lively!" Mr and Mrs
Duck left the house arm in arm.

"Wet feet," wailed Baby.

"Don't dally, dear.
Don't drag behind,"
called Mr Duck.

"Wet face," pouted Baby. "Water in my eyes."

Mrs Duck pranced along. "See how

the rain rolls off your back!"

"Mud," muttered Baby.

"Mud, mud, mud."

"Don't dawdle, dear! Don't lag behind!"

Mr and Mrs Duck skipped ahead.

They waddled. They shimmied.

They hopped in all the puddles.

Baby dawdled. She dallied and

pouted and dragged behind.

She sang a little song.

"I do not like the rain one bit

Splashing down my neck.

Baby feathers soaking wet,

I do not like this mean old day."

"Are you singing?" called Mr and Mrs Duck.

"What a fine thing to do in the rain!"

Baby stopped singing.

Grandpa was waiting at the front door.

He put his arm round Baby.

"Wet feet?" he asked.

"Yes," Baby said.

"Wet face?"

Grandpa asked.

"Yes," Baby said.

"Mud?" Grandpa asked.

"Yes," Baby said. "Mud, mud, mud."

"I'm afraid the rain makes Baby cranky," clucked Mr Duck.

"I've never heard of a duck who doesn't like rain," worried Mrs Duck.

"Oh, really?" Grandpa kissed Baby's cheeks.

Grandpa took Baby's hand.

"Come with me, Baby."

They went upstairs to the attic.

"We are looking for a tall, green bag," Grandpa said.

Finally they found it.

Inside was a beautiful red umbrella.

There were matching boots, too.

"These used to be your mother's," Grandpa whispered. "A long time ago, she was a baby duck who did not like rain."

Baby opened the umbrella.

The boots were just the right size.

Baby and Grandpa marched downstairs.

"My boots!" cried Mrs Duck. "And my bunny umbrella!"

"No, mine!" said Baby.

"You look lovely," said Mrs Duck.

Mr Duck put a plate of pancakes on the table.

After that, Baby and Grandpa went outside.

Pit-pat. Pit-a-pat. Pit-a-pit-a-pat.

Oh, the rain came down.
It poured and poured.
Baby Duck and Grandpa
walked arm in arm
in the rain.

They
waddled.

They
shimmied.

They hopped in all
the puddles.

And Baby Duck sang a new song.

"I really like the rain a lot
Splashing my umbrella.
Big red boots on baby feet,
I really love this rainy day."